CULTURE ENCYCLOPEDIA

PERFORMING ARTS

CULTURE ENCYCLOPEDIA
PERFORMING ARTS

Antony Mason

Mason Crest

Mason Crest Publishers Inc.
370 Reed Road
Broomall, PA 19008
(866) MCP-BOOK (toll free)
www.masoncrest.com
This edition first published in 2003

First published by Miles Kelly Publishing,
Bardfield Centre, Great Bardfield, Essex, CM7 4SL, U.K.
Copyright © Miles Kelly Publishing 2002, 2003

2 4 6 8 10 9 7 5 3 1

ISBN 1-59084-481-5

Author
Antony Mason

Designed and Edited by
Starry Dog Books

Project Editor
Belinda Gallagher

Assistant Editors
Mark Darling, Nicola Jessop, Isla Macuish

Artwork Commissioning
Lesley Cartlidge

Indexer
Jane Parker

Picture Research
Ruth Boardman, Liberty Newton

Color Reproduction
DPI Colour, Saffron Walden, Essex, UK

Printed in China

Contents

Performing Arts

I N ANCIENT Greece, some 18,000 people would pack the seats of giant outdoor theaters to watch actors play out scenes of great tragedies. The excitement of watching performers presenting a story, ballct, or stand-up comedy is just as strong today. But performances no longer have to be presented to live audiences: film preserves them forever, and allows elaborate possibilities through locations, camera angles, and special effects. Through television, we have the performing arts beamed into our own homes. Viewing methods may have changed, but many of the skills and effects of performance would still be familiar to the ancient Greeks.

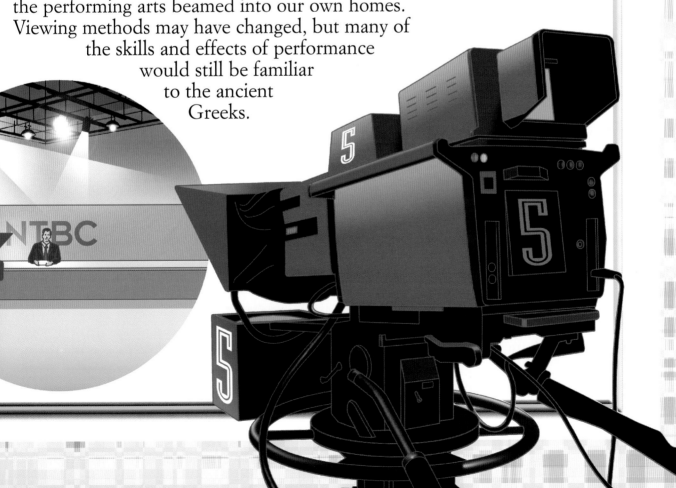

NTBC

Performer and audience

WE are all performers. We perform when we tell a joke or recount a story. Performing is part of human nature. But people who make a living by performing have to be especially good at it. They have to be able to hold the attention of an audience and entertain them; otherwise—quite simply—they will not be paid to perform again. Performing is an ancient craft. Professional entertainers have been making a living by performing since ancient times— earning gifts of money, or perhaps just a meal, at markets, at the courts of kings and nobles, or in specially built theaters. And there have always been storytellers, actors, conjurers, comedians, acrobats, and dancers—just as there are today.

◪ JUGGLERS OF OLD

Tomb paintings from the Etruscan civilization in Italy, dating from more than 2,500 years ago, show a man and a woman juggling. The basic skills of juggling, and the trick of keeping as many objects in the air at the same time, remain the same today.

◪ ELABORATE THEATERS

The earliest theaters, built by the ancient Greeks, were open to the skies. But over time covered theaters developed, and became more elaborate. The King's Theatre, built in 1790, was the largest in London, and one of the grandest. Boxes overlooking the stage gave small parties privacy.

◩ ESCAPOLOGIST

The Hungarian-born American Harry Houdini (1874–1926) was one of the world's greatest showmen, and the most famous "escapologist," or escape artist, of all time. Using clever tricks, he was able to escape from chains and handcuffs while locked in a safe or immersed in a tank of water.

PANTOMIME

English performances known as pantomime are full of fun. Audiences are often encouraged to participate by shouting out warnings to the "good" characters.
The pantomime tradition developed from the Italian comic plays of the 1500s called Commedia dell'Arte.

◩ PROFESSIONAL STORYTELLERS

One of the simplest, oldest, and most effective forms of entertainment is storytelling—an ancient art that has been almost killed off by television. Professional storytellers earned a living by recounting great tales of adventure, love, myth, and heroism. A good storyteller can paint vivid pictures in words, enabling listeners to see characters and scenes in their imaginations.

◩ ENTERTAINING JESTERS

In medieval times, kings and nobles often employed jesters—professional clowns—to provide entertainment by joking and making fun of daily events. Dressed in "motley" (shown here), the jester was a "fool" whom no one took seriously. Because of this, he was able to speak the truth when no one else dared.

◩ VENICE CARNIVAL

The annual Carnival in Venice, Italy, was the most wild and extravagant costume party in Europe during the 1700s, but the French emperor Napoleon put a stop to it when he invaded Italy in 1797. In 1979, the tradition was revived. Hundreds of people dress up in beautiful masks and costumes like these.

The circus

THE circus is one of the oldest forms of popular entertainment. The word "circus" comes from the ancient Greek word for a ring. The round performing area inside a modern circus tent is called an arena, from the Latin for sand. In Roman times, circus arenas were built for chariot races, gladiator fights, and other popular spectacles. During the 18th century, a new kind of circus developed, in which trained horses and other animals were made to perform in the acts. They were soon joined by acrobats and clowns. The shows were originally held indoors, but before long the troupe took to the road, taking their own theater—a tent, or "big top"—with them. Circuses still follow this tradition. Today's circus acts appear more daring, but are actually safe.

◪ COMICAL CLOWNS
No circus is complete without clowns, the comedians of the show. Their comical outfits and facepaint make it immediately clear that they are not going to do anything remotely serious, scary, or even successful. Their humor is almost entirely visual, based on actions, not words. Slapstick humor—throwing foam cakes or custard pies in someone's face, for example—plays a key part in their acts.

◪ ACROBATS
Acrobats, such as these Chinese circus performers, develop their extraordinary skills of balancing, bending, jumping, and tumbling through years of practice. They need strong muscles, very flexible bodies, supreme control, and great courage.

◪ GIANT CIRCUS TENT
Canada's world-famous Cirque du Soleil, founded in 1984, performs in a traditional striped "big top." These giant circus tents are specially designed to be packed up easily for moving to another location. Some are vast: in 1924, 16,700 people packed into a big top to see the Ringling Brothers and Barnum & Bailey Circus, Kansas.

◪ FLYING CIRCUS

A very different kind of circus takes place in the air. Small airplanes can perform stunning aerial acrobatics, looping the loop, going into free falls, and weaving around other airplanes at breathtaking speed. Sometimes, "wing walkers" demonstrate their courage by standing on the wing of the airplane, strapped to a support.

◪ TRADITIONAL CIRCUS

In 1768, Englishman Philip Astley launched a show that included horse-riding acts and acrobats. This kind of traditional circus lasted for some 200 years. Today, animal acts are less popular, and many circuses now have no animals.

HIGH-WIRE ACTS

Daring high-wire acts aim to make the audience fear for the safety of the performer, or tightrope walker (originally, rope was used). With a superb sense of balance, the performer walks high above the ground along a steel cable, which is held taut to give support. Often, a safety net is used.

◪ THE FLYING TRAPEZE

The flying trapeze act was invented in 1859 by the French acrobat Jules Léotard (who gave his name to the gym and dance outfit called a leotard). Performers leap and dive between swings suspended high above the ground. When performing as part of a team, one trapeze artist dangling from a swing will catch another by the hands as the acrobat somersaults through the air.

The origins of drama

STAGE plays, or drama, originated in ancient Greece, where religious festivals of singing, dancing, and acting were held to honor the god Dionysus. Over time, plays written for these festivals became more elaborate. There were two kinds. Tragedies told agonizing, emotionally charged stories about nobles, heroes, and gods. Comedies were usually about ordinary people in funny situations. These same categories have survived to this day. Greek and Roman theaters were open to the skies, but later, plays were performed in any indoor space. The first purpose-built theater with a stage was built in Italy in 1618.

◤ GREEK ACTORS

In ancient Greece, all the actors wore masks. Different kinds of mask represented a certain kind of character. By changing the mask, an actor could play a number of different roles in the same play. All Greek actors were men.

◤ COMMEDIA DELL'ARTE

Italian comic plays known as *Commedia dell'Arte* began in the 1500s. Playing a set of familiar characters —the pretty girl Columbine, her rich old father Pantaloon, Harlequin, and Punch the clown —traveling players entertained the crowds with dance, songs, and slapstick comedy.

◳ MARCEL MARCEAU

Mime is a specialized kind of acting performed entirely without words. Mime artists use movements and gestures to indicate an imaginary world around them. The world's best-known mime artist is Frenchman Marcel Marceau (b. 1923).

KABUKI THEATER
The type of traditional Japanese play called Kabuki developed in the 1700s. It combines richly costumed theater, poetry, singing, music, and dance. No women take part, so men perform the women's roles.

MYSTERY PLAY
In medieval times, worker's guilds presented open-air plays based on stories from the Bible. They were called "mystery plays," but the term really comes from the Latin *ministerium*, a guild or occupation. At religious festivals, different guilds played out episodes from the Bible, from the Creation to Christ's crucifixion.

INDIAN THEATER
The southern Indian tradition of theater called *kathakali* was originally performed in temple ceremonies, and perhaps dates back 2,000 years. The actors, wearing dramatic makeup and rich costumes, tell stories from Hindu mythology, through elaborate dance-like gestures and facial expressions. Training begins at the age of five and lasts for 20 years.

EXAGGERATED STYLE
The greatest British actor in the late 1800s was Henry Irving (1838–1905), here pictured playing the lead role in Shakespeare's *Hamlet*. In the big and busy theaters of Irving's day, actors had to make grand gestures and speak in firm, loud voices—a style that today would be thought "melodramatic," or exaggerated.

Modern theater

U NTIL the late 19th century, most plays were about extraordinary events set in the past, or comedies that poked fun at the way people live. Then a new set of writers began to make dramas about the modern world using situations that the audiences themselves might recognize from their own lives—popularly called "kitchen sink" dramas. Since then, plays have become even more varied. Today, they range from realistic plays that portray a "slice of life," to stylized, antirealistic fantasies that make no attempt to represent real life at all.

◤ STANISLAVSKY

The Russian actor and director Constantin Stanislavsky (1863–1938) revolutionized modern acting. He encouraged actors to work out what their characters would think and feel in the play. This approach is known as "Method Acting."

◀ IBSEN

The Norwegian playwright Henrik Ibsen (1828–1906) is known as the "Founder of Modern Drama." He was the first major dramatist to write about modern people and the social issues of the day. This scene is from his play *Enemy of the People.*

◀ LOOK BACK IN ANGER

When the play *Look Back in Anger* by the British writer John Osborne (1929–94) was first performed in 1956, it caused an outrage. It deals with the conflicts of an ill-matched couple leading an ordinary life. Osborne became known as one of a group of writers called the "Angry Young Men." This scene is from the film of 1959.

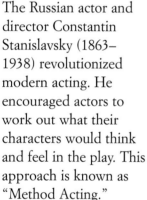

◤ A DIFFERENT VIEWPOINT

The British dramatist Tom Stoppard (b. 1937) first came to notice with his play *Rosencrantz and Guildenstern are Dead* (1966). In this farce, or exaggerated comedy, Stoppard takes a sideways look at Shakespeare's tragedy *Hamlet* by basing his play on two of Shakespeare's characters. Through his clever and often witty writing, he is also able to touch upon serious issues.

◲ SHOCKHEADED PETER

The stage play *Shockheaded Peter* (1998) is a theatrical version of the old German illustrated children's book *Struwelpeter*, which makes vicious fun of old moral tales. The play uses music, puppets, bizarre scenery, and exaggerated performances to re-create the weird world of the original book.

◄ MODERN-DRESS SHAKESPEARE

Old plays can be given a new twist by restaging them in a new era. The plays of William Shakespeare (1564–1616) are often reworked in this way, such as this 1996 version of *A Midsummer Night's Dream*. The effect is to give new meaning to the words. The language is still that of Shakespeare, but a modern setting can show how it is still relevant in the modern world.

Casting to curtain call

GOOD theater needs good performers. A weak play can be made excellent by good actors, and a good play can be ruined by poor or unconvincing acting. Good acting comes from a mixture of natural skill, practice, and experience. But a theatrical performance is really teamwork—from the moment someone has the idea of putting on a play to the final curtain call, when the actors bow at the end of the performance. One of the most important members of the team never appears on stage at all: the director. He or she is responsible for the look of the play and way it is performed.

◢ FINDING THE ACTORS

One of the first tasks in putting on a play is choosing the right actors for the various parts. Actors are invited to an audition by the director, who asks them to read from the script or to perform a short piece on stage. The job of deciding which actor is best suited for each part is called "casting."

◪ THE ROLE OF THE DIRECTOR

Once the director has chosen the actors for the play, rehearsals can begin. At rehearsals, the director guides the actors in how to say their lines and move around the stage. The director also makes decisions about what kind of scenery to use, the style of costumes and the lighting, and coordinates all the people involved. Here, the director is rehearsing a scene from the opera
La Bohème.

◀ THE ROLE OF THE PROMPTER

Almost all actors become nervous before they go on stage, and once in front of an audience they sometimes forget their lines. It is the job of the "prompter," who remains hidden at the side of the stage, to follow the script throughout a performance, and help an actor who "dries up" on stage by whispering the next line. Even the best actors—such as Laurence Olivier and Vivien Leigh, seen here in *Romeo and Juliet*—have needed prompting.

SCRIPT

The very first stage of making a play, usually, is writing the script. A script generally consists of two elements—the speeches and dialogue spoken by the characters, and stage directions, which tell the actors where and when to move.

◤ PRACTICE MAKES PERFECT

Actors attend many rehearsals before a play or film is shown to the public. At rehearsals, the actors and the director work at coordinating words and movements, as well as exits and entrances. The actors give each other "cues," or signals, so that they know when to speak or do something. Here, Barbra Streisand is rehearsing a dance in *Funny Girl* (1968).

◀ TEAMWORK

Many stage shows require teamwork from the cast, particularly if the show includes extravagant musical routines, as in *The Boyfriend* (film version 1971). A special director of dance, called a choreographer, teaches the actors the dance routines. They must work together as a team until they can make it all look smooth and easy!

Inside a theater

PUTTING on a play involves many more people than just the director and the actors. There are set designers and set builders, lighting technicians, costume designers and wardrobe assistants, makeup artists, and stage managers and stage hands who organize the scene changes. Any theater also has "front-of-house" staff, who sell and check the tickets and look after the audience. While the actors come and go, many of the people working backstage and front-of-house are employed permanently by the theater. A theater manager must ensure that a production can cover all its costs, and even make a profit.

◪ SCENERY DESIGN

A play's scenery provides the background setting. Usually painted onto flat screens, it may represent a garden, the inside of a house, or whatever is appropriate. The design may be sumptuous or very sparse, depending on what effect the director wants to create. It must also provide places for the actors to make their entrances and exits.

PROPS

Any moveable object on the stage—such as a gun in a drawer or a letter on a desk—is known as a "prop" (short for "property"). It is the job of the stagehands to make sure that the props are in the right place on stage for the actors to use.

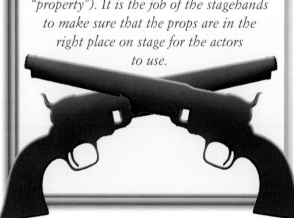

◪ THEATER INTERIOR

A big theater is a highly complex building. The audience sees only a small part of it as they enter through the foyer and find their seat in the auditorium. Behind the stage, which is in the middle of the building, are large areas used for storing scenery, wardrobe rooms for storing costumes, dressing and makeup rooms, rehearsal areas, and a canteen for the actors and stage crew.

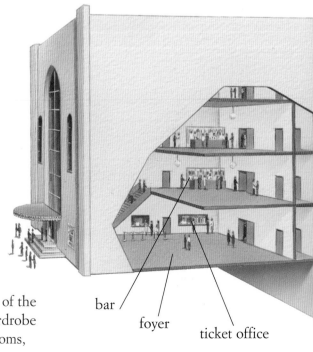

bar

foyer

ticket office

⬛ THE EFFECTS OF LIGHTING

While a play is still in rehearsal, lighting technicians work with the director to plan the lighting for the play very carefully. Different scenes require different effects, from moonlit woodland shadows to a bright interior, a spotlit star, or a sudden flash of lightning. During a performance, most lights are operated from a lighting console, which allows the lighting technician to switch the lights on and off, or change or fade them "on cue," exactly when needed.

◀ COSTUME AND MAKEUP

Actors can be transformed into their characters by their costumes and makeup. Costume designers help to turn the director's vision of how the characters should look into reality. The costumes are either specially made or bought. Makeup artists can also completely change an actor's appearance. The makeup is often applied boldly, because it has to be seen at a great distance and under the glare of the stage lights.

auditorium

stage

rehearsal area

scenery

wardrobe room
(wigs and costumes)

make-up
room

wings

lighting
technician

scenery workshop

Opera and musicals

AN OPERA is a kind of sung drama. The first operas were created in Venice in about 1600. Early operas often related tales from classical mythology, but later works ranged from tales of love and comic misunderstandings, to great tragedies involving trickery, murder, sickness, and war. Of course, in real life people do not go around singing to each other! But opera allows the performers not simply to sing what they want to say, but also to express their innermost thoughts. Musicals offer a more popular and approachable blend of singing and acting, often appealing to a wider audience.

◪ BAYREUTH

The German composer Richard Wagner (1813–83) wrote some of the most magnificent and ambitious operas, most based on German myths. He built a theater to mount these huge productions in his home town of Bayreuth, in Bavaria, and founded the annual festival of his work.

◪ MADAME BUTTERFLY

One of Italy's greatest opera composers Giacomo Puccini (1858–1924) wrote *Madame Butterfly* in 1904, at a time when there was a great interest in Japanese culture in Europe. It tells of a tragic marriage between a Japanese woman and an American naval officer, Lieutenant Pinkerton, and ends in her suicide.

◪ THE MARRIAGE OF FIGARO

Wolfgang Amadeus Mozart (1756–91) wrote this delightful, funny opera in about 1786. Based on a French play of the same name, it relates the complicated love story of a count who tries to steal the girlfriend of his servant, Figaro. Some of the songs are deeply moving.

◪ OKLAHOMA!

The successful partnership between Richard Rodgers (1902–79), who wrote music, and Oscar Hammerstein II (1895–1960), who wrote words, produced some of the best-known American musicals, including *Oklahoma!*, *The King and I*, *South Pacific*, and *The Sound of Music*. Their skill was in combining popular songs with a good story.

◪ PLACIDO DOMINGO

Opera has produced some great stars, who are celebrated for the quality of their voices. They command huge fees to sing at opera houses around the world. One such star is the Spanish tenor Placido Domingo (b. 1941), here seen in a 1983 film version of *La Traviata*, by the great Italian opera composer, Giuseppe Verdi (1813–1901).

◪ LES MISÉRABLES

Early musicals were generally lighthearted, but the huge success of *Les Misérables* (1980), with music by French composer Claude-Michel Schönberg and words by Alain Boublil and Herbert Kretzmer, showed that more serious subjects were possible. Based on the novel by Victor Hugo, it is set during the French Revolution.

ARIAS

Many of the most famous operas contain "songs" sung by one of the lead singers. These are known as arias, *the Italian word for an "air" or "tune." A famous example is the hugely popular "Nessun Dorma," from Puccini's opera* Turandot.

The world of dance

DANCE is one of the oldest of all the performing arts. Traditional dancing has formed part of almost all cultures around the world. No doubt originally it was an activity to participate in, rather than to watch. But early on, dancers developed performances designed to be watched by an audience. While folk dances remain firmly rooted in tradition, new forms of dancing are developing all the time, in response to the kinds of music people like to listen to, and the ways they choose to entertain themselves.

◣ AFRICAN DANCE
Dance in Africa is usually performed to the beat of drums. Many traditional dances were performed for special occasions, such as marriages, harvest, or war. They are often highly energetic.

◢ GREEK TRADITION
Greece has one of the most lively traditions of folk dancing in the modern world. Traditional dancing is still widely performed, especially at weddings. While the traditions of the old folk dances are carefully respected and preserved, Greek dance is constantly changing. The *syrtaki,* for instance, is a new dance, introduced in 1964 through the film *Zorba the Greek.*

◣ ABORIGINAL RITUALS
For the Aborigines of Australia, dance formed a part of religious rituals and ceremonies. There were once more than 500 different Aboriginal tribes, and each had its own distinctive style of dance. Most involved imitations of animals or spirits, and were accompanied by chanting.

WHIRLING DERVISHES

Sufis form a mystical group within Islam, and are found in parts of the Middle East and North Africa. In one of their rituals, they chant the name of God to rhythmic music and clapping, and begin to swirl around in a trancelike state. These dancers are sometimes called "whirling dervishes."

GRACEFUL MOVEMENTS

The traditional dances of the Indonesian island of Bali were mostly all devised for performance at Hindu temple ceremonies. Dancers begin their rigorous training at a very young age— girl dancers are considered to be at their peak aged about 12. The graceful, complex movements are danced to the music of gamelan orchestras.

BREAK DANCING

An acrobatic style of dance developed in New York during the 1980s, as an accompaniment to the new kind of music called rap and hip-hop culture. It involved much more energetic movements than previous dance styles, and greater use of the hands and body on the floor, with spinning and gymnastic floor movements. Tracksuit bottoms and running shoes were part of the standard dress.

BALLROOM DANCING

In the past in Europe, dances and balls gave young men and women a rare opportunity to meet. They learned formal dances, such as the waltz or the polka. The tango (shown here) is a racier type of dance that developed in Argentina in the early 1900s.

P E R F O R M I N G   A R T S

The ballet story

BALLET originated in Italy and France about 300 years ago as stage performances that told a story through movements to music. "Classical ballet" developed into a disciplined style of dancing that required supreme control of the body and dancing on the tips of the toes. All the movements are planned and rehearsed in great detail. A new approach to ballet developed during the 20th century, in which some of the disciplines of classical ballet were dropped to permit more freedom of movement. Good ballet brings together technically superb performance with a convincing artistic interpretation of the music. It produces a mixture of sight and sound that is deeply satisfying to watch, but may be hard to express in words.

◤ ISADORA DUNCAN

Isadora Duncan (1878–1927) developed a style of dancing based on Greek classical dance. Performing barefoot in flowing robes, she introduced free expression, and was highly influential in the development of modern dance.

◁ LA SYLPHIDE

Classical ballet became an international success with *La Sylphide* (1832). It was the work of a bold new generation of dancers, and it demonstrated the charm and artistic beauty of this highly disciplined form of dancing. In the ballet, a Scottish peasant forsakes his bride-to-be for the love of a winged sprite, who represents a happiness he can never attain.

▣ THE RED SHOES

The British film *The Red Shoes* (1948) starring Moira Shearer, tells the story of a young dancer who becomes impassioned by her art, and is saved from obsession by a young composer. Its beautifully filmed dance sequences had a major impact on the British public's appreciation of ballet.

☑ POSITIONS AND POINTS

In classical ballet, all movements end with one of the five positions. These were devised in the 1700s primarily as a way of making the feet look elegant. Classical ballerinas also dance on the tips of their toes, or "points." Their shoes are stiffened to help them.

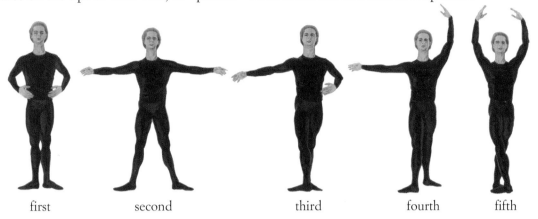

first   second   third   fourth   fifth

BALLETS RUSSES

The Ballets Russes was launched in 1909 by manager Sergei Diaghilev. The mix of modern dance and music often shocked audiences, and even caused a riot in the theater.

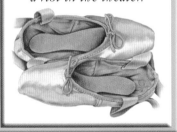

▣ CELEBRATED DANCER

The Russian Vaslav Nijinsky (1890–1950) was one of the most celebrated ballet dancers of all time. He became famous for his dancing with the Ballets Russes. Roles included *L'Aprés-midi d'un faune* ("A faun's afternoon") in 1912. His career was cut short when he became mentally unwell in 1919.

☑ BOLSHOI BALLET

The famous Bolshoi Ballet was founded in Moscow as a dance school in 1773. The Bolshoi Theater was built in 1856. The ballet school is famous for the athletic skills of its dancers, and its large-scale performances— this one is of the 1907 ballet *Les Sylphides,* originally choreographed by Mikhail Fokine (1880–1942).

Powerful puppets

IN INDONESIA, it is still possible to watch huge battle scenes from the great epics of Hindu mythology performed by just one man using an oil lamp, a white screen, and a box full of flat, cut-out puppets on sticks. By contrast, an audience might be moved to tears by a love story performed by two socks on a pair of hands. Puppets can cast this extraordinary range of illusions, and are capable of creating far bigger and stranger stage effects than human actors. They can create theater on a miniature scale and on a grand scale. There are three main kinds of puppets: shadow puppets, glove puppets, and string puppets, or marionettes.

◤ VENTRILOQUISTS

Ventriloquism is the art of speaking without moving the lips, and making the sound appear to come from a puppet, or "dummy." The audience is led to believe that the dummy is having a conversation, or an argument, with the ventriloquist, to comic effect. Here, the ventriloquist is American Edgar Bergen (1903–1978).

◤ INDONESIAN SHADOW PUPPETS

Traditional Indonesian shadow puppets are cut from leather. A stick supports the back and provides a handle for the *dalang* (puppeteer) to hold at the base, while two thin sticks are used to operate the hands. The *dalang* sits behind the screen onto which the shadows are projected, and the audience sits in front of it.

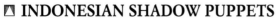

◣ PUNCH AND JUDY

This traditional English form of puppet show, based on the old Italian farces of the *Commedia dell'Arte*, dates back to the 1700s. The stories revolve around the cruel and boastful Mr. Punch and his loud-mouthed wife Judy. Although performed for children, at parties, or at the beach, the comic story involves the death of a baby, wife-beating, murder, and imprisonment.

◨ MARIONETTES

String puppets, or marionettes, like this one from Thailand, hang on strings from an X-shaped pair of bars. The puppeteer holds the bars with one hand, allowing the puppet to dangle onto a small stage. The other hand operates the strings, which are usually attached to the hands, knees, feet, and back.

◨ ANIMATRONICS

In recent decades, puppets have become much more complex. "Animatronics"—remote-control electronics assisted by computers—are used to animate, or bring alive, a puppet (often an animal). The puppet builders and operators can move many tiny parts of the puppet, such as its facial features. Famous animatronic film creatures include the gremlins.

PINOCCHIO

The famous Italian tale about a naughty puppet called Pinocchio was first written in 1883 by the author known as Collodi. The puppet, made from a magical piece of wood, laughs and cries like a child. Pinocchio soon shows his maker that he has a life of his own, and goes off on all kinds of strange adventures.

◨ THE MUPPETS

The world's most popular puppets of recent years are the Muppets, created by America's Jim Henson (1936–90). They are essentially glove puppets with rods attached to the arms. Kermit the Frog, the first character, was invented in 1955, followed by many others, including blonde Miss Piggy. The Muppet Show (1976–81) was watched by 235 million people worldwide.

Origins of motion pictures

WHEN the French brothers Auguste and Louis Lumière made the first-ever movie in 1895, they had no idea that they were laying the foundations of one of the great modern art forms. But it soon became clear that cinema could offer an inexpensive and exciting alternative to theater. The early movies (mostly comedies) were "silent," and so could be enjoyed by audiences around the world, regardless of language. Soon, however, directors realized that film was not simply a way to create mass entertainment—it could also be a means of serious artistic expression.

◢ EADWEARD MUYBRIDGE

Early photographers looked for a way to take photos that gave the impression of movement. In the 1880s, Eadweard Muybridge (1830–1904) set up groups of cameras with threads attached to the shutters, so movement could be recorded in quick succession. After printing the photographs, he ran them together in his "zoepraxiscope," which gave the impression of motion, similar to this early French film.

◀ CINÉMATOGRAPHE

Photographers knew that they could create the illusion of motion by making and showing numerous pictures one after the other. But they did not have the means to do this until the Lumière brothers invented the "cinématographe," a device that combined the camera and the projector.

▣ CHARLIE CHAPLIN

Movies were silent until 1927. Instead of speaking, the actors told the story through mime. The occasional sentence of text would also appear on a black screen, giving the audience a hint about the plot. Comedy was one of the most popular forms of the silent cinema, and the greatest star was the English actor Charlie Chaplin (1889–1977). He acted the part of the "little tramp" in numerous movies, such as *The Kid* (1921), and could be hilarious, idiotic, cunning, and pathetic.

EARLY PROJECTORS

One of the great breakthroughs of motion pictures was projecting pictures onto a screen, imitating a theater. In fact, projectors had been invented for motion picture shows, even before the invention of film.

◨ GREAT WESTERN TRAIN ROBBERY

One of the very first types of American motion picture was the Western. *The Great Train Robbery* was made in 1903, just eight years after motion pictures were invented. At this time, no film lasted much longer than 10 minutes. They were shown to the public in traveling shows and makeshift halls.

◨ SILENT STAR

One of the greatest stars of the silent movie era was the Italian-American Rudolph Valentino (1895–1926). He played romantic leads in films such as *The Sheikh* (1921), and was nicknamed "the Great Lover." When he died suddenly aged just 31, some 80,000 emotional mourners paid their respects as his body lay in state in New York.

◨ CELLULOID

The key to the development of films was celluloid—a continuous strip of flexible plastic film that was stored on reels, like this one of 1931. Celluloid was first used to make motion pictures in 1889. First, a quick succession of photographs was taken using the film. Then light was projected through the developed film onto the screen. Before celluloid, it was not possible to run pictures one after the other so effectively.

Color and special effects

EARLY film makers knew that they could only really compete with theater if they added sound to their films. This was achieved in 1927, when the *The Jazz Singer*, starring Al Jolson, was released—it was the first "talkie." In fact, not everyone welcomed sound. Some of the stars of the silent movies lost their jobs because they had unsuitable voices. And audiences had to learn to be quiet to listen to the film. Another major development was the introduction of color a few years later. Recently, the use of computer-generated images for special effects has had great impact on film making.

◤ FIRST COLOR MOVIE
Early film makers made hand-colored movies as early as 1896. But the first movie in Three-Color Technicolor film was *Becky Sharp* (1935), starring Miriam Hopkins.

▣ BATTLESHIP POTEMKIN
Some early film makers realized that they could create powerful effects using a technique called "montage"—putting together different shots so that they cut from one to the next in quick succession. This was very effectively done in the Russian film *Battleship Potemkin* (1925).

▣ SPACESHIPS
Models and computer technology are used to create some stunning visual effects, such as the huge spaceship in *Independence Day* (1996). Developments in this field have been rapid since the success of films such as *2001: A Space Odyssey* (1968) and the *Star Wars* trilogy (from 1977). Now, if the effects are not entirely convincing, audiences do not bother to see the movie.

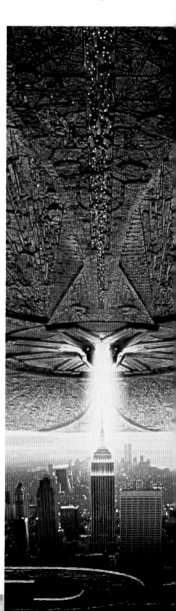

◤ CLOSE UP SHOTS
Film makers soon realized that film had certain advantages over theater. A close up shot, for example, allows the actor to convey subtle changes of emotions. This close up is of actress Michelle Pfeiffer.

◨ STUNT ACTION

A leading actor cannot risk getting hurt in an action scene. So the director uses a specialist stunt actor to take the star's place. The stunt actor is trained to crash cars, jump from moving trains, or leap through fire— and do it safely, as in this scene from the action film *Blown Away* (1994).

◪ SINKING SHIP

For the famous Hollywood blockbuster *Titanic* (1997), starring Leonardo di Caprio and Kate Winslet, computer-generated animation was used for many of the outside shots of the ship. But for the scenes of the sinking, the stars had to perform in thousands of gallons of real water!

LOUIS B. MAYER

One of the great early Hollywood producers was the Russian-born American Louis B. Mayer (1885–1957). He founded Metro-Goldwyn-Mayer (MGM) in 1924.

Making movies

IT IS SAID that film is the most complete of all the art forms, because it combines acting, visual images, music, and often dance. All these elements have to be carefully brought together on strips of celluloid—a process that requires a great deal of organization and large sums of money. A film usually starts as a film script. The director has to be able to visualize the written words so that he or she can turn them into images on screen. Filming is only part of the process. Once complete, the film has to be edited and combined with a soundtrack of voices, music, and noises that go with any special effects.

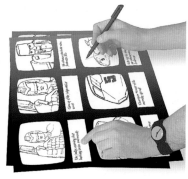

◨ STORYBOARD

A director may plan a film using a "storyboard"— a sequence of sketches that show roughly how each scene will look. This visual record also helps to ensure that small details remain constant throughout the filming.

◪ LEARNING THE SCRIPT

Film actors learn their words from a script, just as stage actors do. But in film making, the scenes are often shot in the wrong order and are edited into the right order later. So actors—like Marilyn Monroe, seen here in *Gentlemen Prefer Blondes* (1953)— learn their parts scene-by-scene.

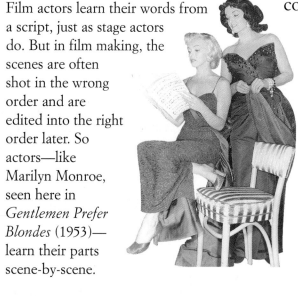

◪ THE POWER OF LIGHTING

Lighting plays a major part in the "look" of a film, whether it is shot outdoors on location, or indoors on a studio set. Backlighting is used here to dramatic effect in a scene from *A Clockwork Orange* (1971), by director Stanley Kubrick (1928–99).

HOLLYWOOD

◥ THE HOME OF FILM

In 1911, pioneer film makers went to a remote settlement called Hollywood, near Los Angeles, to film Westerns, because it had a suitably dry, scrubby landscape. Within two years, it had become the center of American film making and it has dominated the industry worldwide ever since.

◤ THE DIRECTOR

A director's task is to oversee every aspect of the way a movie is made—from scriptwriting, directing the actors on set, and checking how the filming looks through the camera to the final editing. Woody Allen (b. 1935) is seen here paying close attention.

SOUND

In the very early days of cinema, some film makers played gramophone records to accompany their films. But the key to "talkies" was in having a soundtrack that was synchronized with the images.

◪ FILMING ON LOCATION

Film makers can build sets in a film studio that look just like a real street, palace, mountainside, or anything else. But often it is easier, cheaper, and visually more effective to film "on location," using the scenery and buildings of a real place. This is usually the case when a film is set in a foreign country, as with *The Last Emperor* (1987), which was filmed in China. The film makers shoot the outdoor scenes on location, and the indoor scenes in studios back home.

Television

L IKE film before it, television has had a major impact on the performing arts. Since its invention in the 1940s, television has provided thousands of new jobs for actors, directors, and all the technicians involved in the performing arts. Television has also helped to spread knowledge and understanding about all the arts—including classical music, ballet, painting, theater, and poetry—to everyone who has a television. New kinds of performing arts have been created specially for the television, such as soap operas, low-budget TV movies, and pop videos. But many people will argue that television can never replace the thrill of watching the performing arts presented live and in person.

◩ COSTUME DRAMAS

Television has been able to attract audiences of millions to subjects like historical dramas by showing them in weekly episodes. "Costume dramas," as they are called, retell in film the stories of the great classics of literature, by writers such as Thomas Hardy. Many foreign television companies broadcast the productions in translation.

◩ THE FIRST TV

The British inventor John Logie Baird (1888–1946) gave the first demonstration of a television in 1925. His apparatus included a cookie tin and darning needles. The system remained fairly basic until the 1950s. Broadcasts were in black and white, and usually performed live. Color was introduced in 1953, but was only used widely from the 1960s.

◪ FRIENDS

TV program makers like to produce series that they can sell to as many TV networks as possible. The American comedy *Friends* is one of the most successful ever, running to nine series since it was launched in 1994. Each actor was reported to be earning US $700,000 per episode in the final series.

VIDEO
Camcorders allow people to make their own films easily. The films have a special "hand-held" quality that is now sometimes imitated in Hollywood movies.

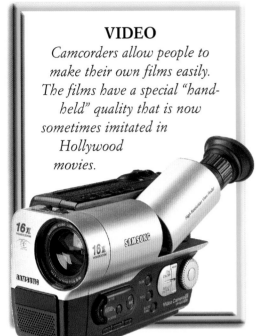

◪ BRAZILIAN SOAPS
Soap operas are serialized dramas, presented regularly on television. They usually relate day-to-day dramas in the lives of ordinary people. Brazil produces a large number of soaps, called "telenovelas," which are popular throughout the Portuguese and Spanish-speaking world. The actors are major stars in Brazil.

◪ TELEVISION STUDIO
Filming for television is often done from a studio. A number of TV cameras are used at the same time. These send pictures to a control room, where the images are selected for transmission. This process has to be done very quickly for live broadcasts. The same studio may be used for a variety of programs, so the space has to be adaptable.

◪ SATELLITE
TV pictures and sound can be sent rapidly around the world. They are transmitted to satellites in stationary orbit in space, and then redirected to another part of the world. This means that live news pictures can be broadcast immediately from any trouble spots, making the world seem a smaller place.

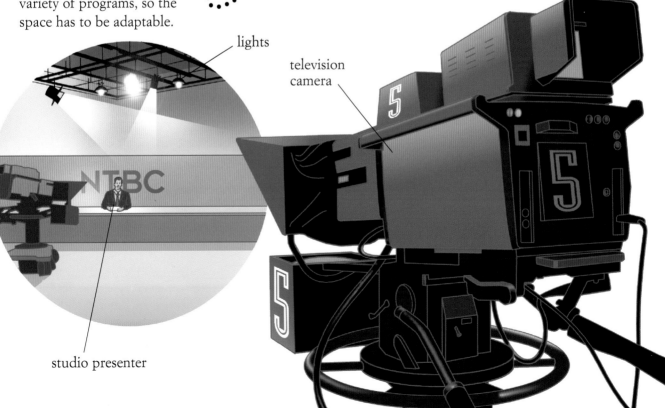

lights

television camera

studio presenter

Glossary

ANIMATRONICS
The techniques of designing, building, and operating lifelike machines or robots which are worked by electronics, assisted by computers, and controlled remotely, to mimic real people, animals, or aliens.

AUDITION
An interview to find suitable performers for roles in a play or musical performance. It usually involves candidates reading from a script, singing, or giving a short performance, watched by the director.

AUDITORIUM
The main part of a theater, or public performance venue, where the audience sits to view the stage. It may consist of a floor area, with seats called stalls, and layers called circles and balconies above, also with seats.

BROADCAST
To scatter or spread something over a wide area—today this word usually refers to the spreading of information, news, or knowledge by radio or television.

CAST
A list of characters in a play, opera, or similar production, and the names of the actors who play them. Decisions by the director and others about which actor suits each role is called casting.

CELLULOID
An early synthetic plastic, used for billiard balls, dentures, combs, and photographic film. It is highly flammable and has been replaced by less-flammable cellulose acetate for movie film, but the term "celluloid" is still used generally to mean movies or films in the cinema.

CHARIOTS
Wheeled vehicles, usually horse-drawn, invented about 5,000 years ago for fast travel and particularly warfare. Soldiers, especially Romans, also raced chariots as sport to show off their skills and bravery.

CHOREOGRAPHER
The person who decides which dance steps and movements should be used by people during a ballet, musical, or similar production, and then directs the performance of the dancers.

CIVILIZATION
Large groups of people that live together in towns and cities, and who all share the same or similar culture, traditions, laws, and government.

CONJURER
A person who skilfully performs tricks using fast hand movements (sleight of hand), special objects or props, and other deceptions, so that watchers cannot see how they happen and so the tricks seem like magic.

CUE
Words or actions of a performer which alert other performers that is their turn to speak or carry out certain actions.

DIALOGUE
A conversation or discussion between two actors in a play or production, or between two representatives of groups with different ideas.

ESCAPOLOGIST
A person who designs tricks or illusions where he or she is put into a serious or life-threatening situation, with no apparent means of escape, but manages to get free.

ETRUSCANS
Ancient Mediterranean people who thrived in central Italy for hundreds of years, but who were eventually overpowered by the Romans.

FARCE
A type of play or production, where comedy is exaggerated and based on ludicrous and improbable situations, events, and misunderstandings.

FOLK DANCE
The traditional dance of a group of people or a country. Its movements and steps are passed down from generation to generation, and often performed in traditional costume.

FOYER
The entrance hall of a theater, or performance venue, where the audience comes into the building, perhaps meet in groups, and buy tickets, programs, refreshments, and merchandise. Also known as "front of house."

GAMELAN
A traditional type of orchestra from the Indonesian islands of Java and Bali, with a wide range of instruments made mainly of bronze.

GLADIATORS
Men trained to fight each other or wild animals and provide a bloodthirsty spectacle, especially for the huge audiences attending the arenas in ancient Rome.

GUILDS
Associations dating from medieval times, formed by the craftspeople, traders, or merchants, to protect work and maintain standards. Guilds provided apprenticeships to train young people.

LOCATION
A site outside a movie studio, where actors and crew film parts of a movie that need specialized backgrounds and scenery, and the buildings of real places.

MEDIEVAL
Usually referring to the Middle or Dark Ages, a 1,000-year period which generally began at the end of the Roman era, around AD 400, and ended with the Renaissance period, around AD 1400.

MORAL
Knowing the difference between right and wrong, good and bad, what is acceptable, and how to treat other people.

MYSTERY PLAYS
Medieval dramas usually about stories from the Bible, especially those about Christ, performed under the direction of the Church, but later by town guilds.

MYTHOLOGY
Collections of traditional stories used to describe and explain the history of a people or group, quite often involving gods, goddesses, and heroes and heroines.

PROMPTER
A person hidden from the audience just offstage, who follows the script of a play or production, as the actors say their lines, and reminds or "prompts" them if they forget what they have to say or do.

REHEARSAL
Preparation for a public performance, such as playing a piece of music or acting in a play, by practicing over and over again.

SATELLITE
An object that goes around and around, or orbits, another object. The Moon is the natural satellite of the Earth. Communications satellites also orbit the Earth but they are artificial (man-made).

STATIONARY ORBIT (GEOSTATIONARY ORBIT)
An artificial satellite circling the Earth in the same direction and at the same speed as the Earth turns, so that it seems to "hover" above a place on Earth's surface.

SYNCHRONIZED
When things happen at the same time or in a set pattern. For example, in films, the sound recording runs alongside the film so that the actors' words are heard precisely when their lips move—words and movements are "in synch."

TRADITION
The passing on of the culture of a group of people from old to young, including their customs, stories, history, and beliefs.

TRAGEDY
A very sad event, such as an unhappy love affair or an appalling crime or a disaster. In theater, the term refers to a play about a sequence of unhappy events which usually end for the worst.

TRANSMISSION
The transferring or moving of something from one place to another. Today, it usually refers to the sending out or broadcasting of the radio signals for a radio or television program or sending signals along cables.

TRIBE
A group of people who share the same history, traditions, values, and customs, and usually live in the same territory. Members of a tribe may also share a common ancestry.

TV NETWORK
A large group of broadcasting stations, operated by a single organization, which are linked so that they can send out, or broadcast, the same programs over a large area, such as an entire country or continent.

VENTRILOQUISM
The skill of speaking without moving the lips and "throwing the voice," so that it sounds as though it comes from somewhere else, such as from a box or from the mouth of a dummy.

WESTERN MOVIES
Films about people exploring and settling in western North America, mainly in the 19th and early 20th centuries, especially people descended from the European arrivals in North America, their struggles against the elements and their dealings with the Native American peoples (Indians). The movies can be fictional or based on fact and usually involve cowboys, horseriding, cattle ranching, outlaws, and gunfights.

WING WALKERS
People who take part in aerial acrobatic displays—by climbing out of the main airplane onto the wings and perform maneuvers such as dances or somersaults.

ZOEPRAXISCOPE
A device that gives the illusion of a moving image, when a series of pictures on the inside of a spinning cylinder are viewed through vertical slits in the cylinder.

Index

PERFORMING ARTS

ACKNOWLEDGMENTS

Art Archive: Page 8 (t/r) Etruscan Necropolis Tarquinia/Dagli Orti, (c) Eileen Tweedy, 9 (t/r) Galleria d'Arte Moderna Udine Italy/Dagli Orti, 12 (c/l) Musée Bonnat Bayonne France/Dagli Orti, 13 (t/l) Art Archive, 18 (t/r) Francesco Venturi, 20 (t/r) Richard Wagner Museum Bayreuth/Dagli Orti, 24 (c/l) Victoria and Albert Museum, London/Eileen Tweedy **Corbis:** Page 13 (c/l) Hulton-Deutsch Collection, 15 (c/r) Robbie Jack, 16 (t/r) Hulton-Deutsch Collection, (b) Ira Nowinski, 19 (t/l) Hulton-Deutsch Collection, 20 (b) Robbie Jack (cont'd page 21), 22 (c/l) Penny Tweedie, (b) Gunter Marx, 25 (b) Robbie Jack, 28 (t/r) Hulton-Deutsch Collection, 29 (b) Bettmann, 35 (t/r) Stephanie Maze **Kobal:** Page 14 (b) Kobal Collection, 15 (t/r) Kobal Collection, (b/l) Kobal Collection, 17 (t/l) Kobal Collection, (t/r) Columbia, (b/r) EMI/MGM, 21 (t/l) Magna Theatres, (t/r) Aceent/RAI, (c/r) Konow Rolph/Mandalay, 24 (b/r) Rank, 26 (t/r) Kobal Collection, 27 (t/r) Warner Bros, (b/r) Jim Henson Productions, 29 (t/r) Edison, 30 (t/r) Kobal Collection, (c) Kobal Collection, (b/l) Tursi, Mario/20th Century Fox, (b/r) Kobal Collection, 31 (c/l) Kobal Collection, (r) Kobal Collection, 32 (c/l) 20th Century Fox, (b) Warner Bros, 33 (c) United Artists, 33 (b) Columbia, 34 (b) Joey Delvalle

All other photographs are from:
MKP Archives; Corel Corporation; Photodisk

Other titles in this series:
Art • Design • History of Culture • Literature
Music • Myths and Legends • Religion